ALFIE
Alfie Outdoors

Shirley Hughes

THE BODLEY HEAD
LONDON

The sun was up early
and so was Alfie,
out in the back garden,
before anyone else
was properly awake,
not even Annie Rose.

The birds were busy
and so was Alfie,
checking his secret hiding place
in the bush where he sometimes kept a shop.

And high in the sky,
way above the roof tops and T.V. aerials,
some fluffy white clouds were drifting slowly,
like a flock of sheep across the blue.

It was going to be a lovely day.

ALFIE

Alfie Outdoors

To Leah with love and gratitude

Other titles in the Alfie series:

Alfie Gets in First
Alfie's Feet
Alfie Gives a Hand
An Evening at Alfie's
Alfie and the Birthday Surprise
Alfie Wins a Prize
Alfie and the Big Boys
Alll About Alfie
Alfie's Christmas

Alfie Weather
Alfie's World
Annie Rose is my
Little Sister
Rhymes for Annie Rose
The Big Alfie and Annie Rose
Storybook
The Big Alfie Out of Doors
Storybook

ALFIE OUTDOORS
A BODLEY HEAD BOOK 978 1 782 30031 1

Published in Great Britain by The Bodley Head, an imprint of Random House Children's Publishers UK
A Penguin Random House Company

Penguin
Random House
UK

This edition published 2015

1 3 5 7 9 10 8 6 4 2

Copyright © Shirley Hughes, 2015

The right of Shirley Hughes to be identified as the author of this work has been asserted in accordance with the Copyright, Designs and Patents Act 1988.

Penguin Random House is committed to a sustainable future for our business, our readers and our planet.
This book is made from Forest Stewardship Council® certified paper.

MIX
Paper from
responsible sources
FSC® C018179

RANDOM HOUSE CHILDREN'S PUBLISHERS UK
61–63 Uxbridge Road, London W5 5SA

www.randomhousechildrens.co.uk   www.randomhouse.co.uk   www.alfiebooks.co.uk

Addresses for companies within The Random House Group Limited can be found at: www.randomhouse.co.uk/offices.htm

THE RANDOM HOUSE GROUP Limited Reg. No. 954009

A CIP catalogue record for this book is available from the British Library.

Printed in China

As soon as he was dressed, Alfie wandered down to the end
of the garden to take a look around. Right at the bottom
there was a straggly patch where Mum had her washing line,
and there was a little shed where Dad kept his gardening things.

It was a good place to play, or to go if you wanted to be
on your own for a bit.

But this morning he found Dad there. He was leaning on his spade and looking at the ground. Alfie looked at the ground too, but he could not see anything interesting there.

"Do you know what, Alfie?" said Dad. "I'm thinking that if I dug this patch over, we could grow vegetables here."

Alfie laughed because he knew that vegetables really came from the supermarket in packets. But Dad told him that they had to grow in the ground, long before anyone can pick them and put them in a shop.

"You could grow something too, if you like," said Dad. "But first we'd have to dig this soil over to make it nice and welcoming for the seeds when we plant them."

Alfie did not think that digging was very
exciting unless you were at the seaside.
But after a while he fetched his spade
from the sandpit and began to dig too.

This digging turned out to be more interesting than he thought it would be, because under the soil a lot of creepy crawlies were living. There were interesting creatures like ants, earwigs, wriggling worms and snails in their beautiful shell houses.

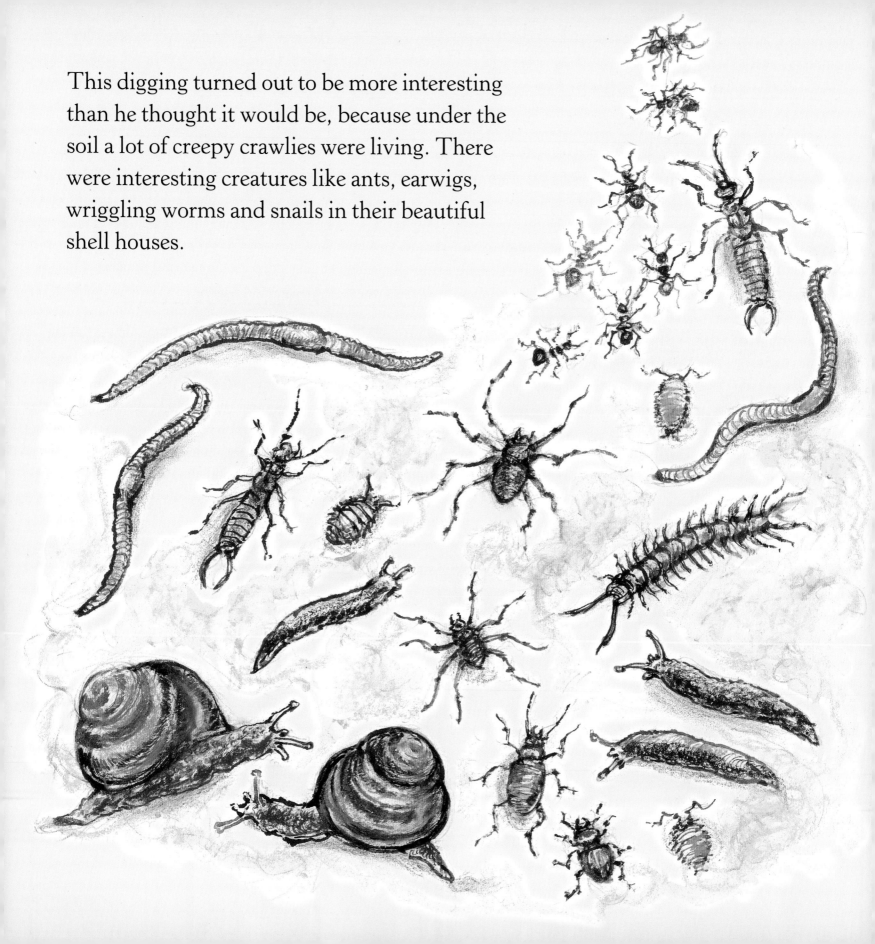

Alfie liked creepy crawlies. He crouched down to watch a whole army of ants pushing and pulling a piece of twig along. It was much bigger than they were. Alfie wondered where they were trying to take it and what they would do with it when they got there.

Soon Mum called Alfie indoors to have his breakfast and then it was time for him to go to nursery school.

When he got back he ran straight into the garden to find Dad. He was still digging. He had made quite a big space, which was covered with freshly turned-over earth. He picked out all the stones and bits of rubbish and broken plant pots and piled them up. Alfie found a little racing car he thought he had lost and a wheel from Annie Rose's old doll's buggy.

Dad put all the dead leaves into the special place where he kept
his grass cuttings. Then he and Alfie made a bonfire of all the
other rubbish. That was the best bit of all.

On Saturday morning Mum, Dad, Alfie and Annie Rose drove to the garden centre, where they loaded up a trolley with all kinds of pot plants.

"Would you like a packet of seeds of your own to grow?" Dad asked Alfie. "You could plant them in your special vegetable patch."

Alfie chose carrot seeds. He did not specially like carrots himself, but he thought he knew someone who might.

When they got home Dad helped Alfie to
scatter his seeds in his own special corner
of the vegetable garden where they would
get plenty of sun. Then they got out the
hosepipe and Dad let Alfie spray his seeds
with water.

At bedtime Alfie was very wet and
muddy. "You're a real gardener now,"
said Mum.

Alfie very much wanted his carrots to grow quickly because he planned to take one to the goat sanctuary, which was one of his favourite places. It was where goats who had no home could go to live together and be well looked after. Mum and Dad took him there quite often.

Alfie's special friend among the goats was Gertrude, a lovely grey and white lady goat. She always stuck out her neck and her big snuffly nose through the fence, waiting to be stroked and hoping for something to eat. Alfie wished he could tell her that soon he would be bringing her one of his own special carrots which he had grown himself.

Every day Alfie went down to the vegetable patch to see if his carrots were growing. But there was no sign of them. When Alfie's friend Bernard came to play he looked too. But he could not see any carrots either. It was very disappointing.

"I don't think much of this gardening stuff," said Bernard.

So they ran off and kicked a ball around.
Then they played at being fierce monsters,
lurking in the bushes and jumping out at
each other.

Alfie had more or less given up on checking his carrot seeds, when one day Dad called him to come and have a look. And they saw some little green shoots coming up where the seeds had been planted.

Alfie's seeds were beginning to grow!

Alfie was very excited. But the carrots took their time.
Every day Alfie went to water them and cheer them on.
"Grow, carrots, grow!" he told them.

At last Dad said he thought
the carrots were ready to pick.
Alfie pulled up a beautiful big
one for Gertrude.

He washed it carefully
and wrapped it in newspaper,
and they all set out for the
goat sanctuary.

But when they got there, and Alfie ran up
to the fence to look for Gertrude, he could
not see her anywhere!

They asked one of the helpers who looked after the goats where Gertrude was, and she told them that Gertrude had somehow managed to get out through the fence and was missing! But she said that she was sure she had not strayed far away and would soon be found.

When they got back Alfie cried at
bedtime, thinking of Gertrude out
there somewhere alone in the dark
and not being able to find her
way home.

Next morning he was so sad that he
did not want to play with Annie Rose
or help Dad in the vegetable patch.

He moped about the garden miserably.
Then he took Flumbo and crawled
into his special place inside a bush
and would not come out.

Mum telephoned the goat sanctuary,
but there was still no news of Gertrude.
   Alfie was in the bath when the
telephone rang. Dad took the call.
As soon as he had finished he let out
a whoop of joy and ran upstairs.

"Gertrude has been found!" he shouted.
"She was in somebody's back garden eating their
lettuces! And what's more, she had pulled their
clean washing off the line!"

Alfie was very happy when he
heard the news. He did not care
a bit that Gertrude had pulled
down the silly old washing.

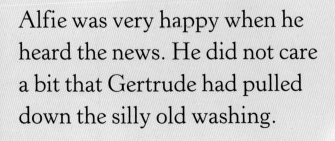

Next morning he and Dad
pulled up another beautiful
carrot for Gertrude, and
they all set out once again
for the goat sanctuary.

When they arrived, there she was! And when Alfie held
out the carrot she came straight over and started to munch.
Alfie was very pleased.

When they got home Alfie and Dad went down to have a last look at their vegetable garden.

"Gertrude liked my carrot a lot, didn't she?" said Alfie.

"She sure did," said Dad. "When we next go to the garden centre I'll buy you some more seeds if you like. And you can choose what you'd like to grow next."

July

August

September

October

November

December